LINGER

A Short Story

MELISSA J. CRISPIN

Copyright © 2022 by Melissa J. Crispin

ISBN: 978-0-9600645-4-0 (print)

ISBN: 978-0-9600645-3-3 (ebook)

Published by Angry Eyebrow Press

Cover art by Melissa J. Crispin

For the hopeless romantics that believe love conquers all.

The ocean waves lapped against the shore. My lips split into a wide smile as I sat on the deck and soaked in the perfect summer day. Noah tossed Faith's blue ball toward the water and she eagerly chased after it, her tail whipping back and forth like crazy. Laughter and happy barks filled my ears while I twirled the ice in my drink and admired the view.

Sure, the beach was gorgeous, but it paled in comparison to the shirtless guy on the sand below me. Noah's olive skin glistened, beads of water running down his chiseled chest and continuing past a well-defined six pack. He ran one hand through his toffee-colored locks and glanced up in my direction, his hazel eyes finding mine.

My fiancé. It would take a while to get used to calling him that, and by the time I grew accustomed to it, he'd be my husband. My heart swelled, the grin on my face widening even more.

"Everyone's going to think you're pregnant. You know that, right?" Marlene asked.

"What?" I arched an eyebrow at my soon-to-be sister-in-law. "Why?"

"People don't get married when they're twenty, Tracey. I'm sure you've noticed your friends aren't getting hitched left and right."

That was true enough. My friends were yet to land serious relationships, so getting engaged wouldn't be under consideration in their near future.

Noah climbed the steps and approached the back of my chair, wrapping his arms around my shoulders and planting a kiss on my cheek. "Yeah, well, who cares what anyone thinks? Not many people meet their soulmate when they're twelve, either."

Marlene shrugged. "Things won't always be easy. Take it from this bitter old lady."

Noah slid into the chair beside me. "Oh, I don't know, Sis. You seem like you're doing alright to me. If you ask me, your divorce was Brady's loss. You didn't want the same things in life, so you parted ways. Better now than later. And, by the way, thirty isn't old."

"You're a good little brother." She leaned over and ruffled his hair.

"Try to keep that in mind when you're annoyed about your little brother and his wife living happily ever after in your basement."

Marlene shook her head. "The house is yours as much as it's mine. You read the letter Mom and Dad left with the will. It was placed in my name only because you were too young when the accident happened. You and Tracey living with me, it allows me to fulfill their wishes."

Noah rolled his eyes. "Don't you go getting all sappy. It won't be long until we're on our feet and looking for a place of our own, anyway."

"I have a good feeling about the job interview I went on yesterday," I added. "If I get it, we'll be making enough money every month to move out."

"Really, guys?" Marlene gestured to the house. "This is too much living space for one person, lonely even. Stay as long as you need. I mean it." She turned to me, a conspiratorial expression on her face. "So, you're seriously not pregnant? Come on, you can tell me."

I laughed. "No. Just hopelessly in love." I sipped my drink.
Marlene sighed. "You guys are so cute it's annoying."

I blinked at myself in the full-length mirror, smoothing my hands
down the white gown that hugged my curves and nearly touched the
floor. It was a sleeveless number, the neckline plunging low to form a
'V'. A thin strip of rhinestones stretched below the bodice, giving it
the perfect amount of bling.

"Do you think it looks okay?" I had been lucky to find a dress in my
size on the clearance rack at the bridal shop. It didn't need a stitch of
alterations either, which had to be a small miracle in itself.

"The dress? Are you kidding? It's gorgeous," Marlene said, fanning
out various cosmetics on a nearby dresser. "Come, sit down. I want to
help you with your hair and makeup." I complied. She picked up an
eyeliner pencil and applied color beneath my eyes. "Bronze will make
those big brown eyes of yours pop. And we'll add golden tones to your
eyelids as a complement."

"Thanks for helping me get ready." I meant it more than she probably knew. On a day where Mom would have definitely been around
to help, it was nice to have another woman there for support.

Marlene brushed color on my cheeks. "I'm happy to do it. You're
already like a sister to me. After today, it'll be official." She fussed with
my hair next, twisting it on top of my head, letting soft black curls
cascade down to frame my face. "I'm still surprised that you and Noah

didn't want a church wedding and a reception." She wrestled a bobby pin into place. "Hold your breath." The telltale sound of an aerosol can hissed as Marlene sprayed my updo.

I coughed. "I think that's good." Flailing my hands, I waved her away while also attempting to disperse the chemicals in the air around me. "We didn't see the point in spending all that money when we could use it for so many other things." I rubbed shiny gloss on my pouty lips and picked up the waterproof mascara. "And I'm tired of explaining to everyone that I'm not pregnant. I don't need to spend the evening with everyone searching for my baby bump." I sighed.

Marlene nodded, a smirk on her face. "See? Told you so."

"Doesn't anyone believe in love anymore?"

Many of my friends and Noah's had reacted to our engagement with furrowed brows, along with the nagging question, "Why?" To which I countered, "Why not?" I looked at it from a different perspective entirely. While they were busy highlighting things we'd be missing, I counted everything we would gain.

A hard knock on the basement door made me jump, jerking my hand to the side and causing me to nearly poke my eye out. It creaked opened.

"Noah, you better not come down here. It's bad luck to see the bride before the wedding." I blotted at the corner of one eye with a tissue, wiping away a dark smudge of mascara. But, regardless of my words, he came thundering down the stairs.

"Nice. Way to ignore the bride's wishes," Marlene said.

"Aw, come on. You girls don't believe in that nonsense, do you?"

I shrugged. "I wanted to surprise you."

When his hazel gaze met mine, butterflies fluttered in my stomach. Eight years of staring into those eyes, and every time still punched me in the feels. "You look beautiful." He stalked toward me and rested his hands on my hips. "And I wouldn't be surprised, even if you did make me wait, because you always look beautiful to me."

The corners of my mouth turned up, even though I wanted to pretend to be mad.

"There's the cute annoying thing again," Marlene said. She added in fake gagging for good measure.

Another set of footsteps followed. "Now you wait one minute. First of all, I haven't given her away yet. Second, the justice of the peace wants you out on the sand. It's time to get started." Dad pointed at the back door.

"Fine, I'll go, but not without my best man," Noah said to Marlene.

"Stop calling me that." She grumbled, but the light tone of her voice gave away her true feelings.

The two of them crossed the room. Noah ushered his sister out the door and stepped out onto the beach after her, closing the door softly behind him.

"So, you're sure about him?" Dad asked, playfully nudging my shoulder.

"Am I sure about—" I lifted my hands and made air quotes—" 'the son you never had?' Um, yeah."

Dad laughed. "Okay, good. Felt like it was my fatherly duty to ask. And, I must say I completely agree with him about the way you look. My beautiful girl, all grown up. If only your mother could see you now." Sadness flashed over his face before he replaced it with a firm smile.

"I like to think that she can see us, and that she's with us now." I took a very deep breath, and then blew it out slowly, pulling the veil into place. "Are you ready to walk me down the aisle?"

My favorite song of all time, *A Thousand Years* by Christina Perri, played out of a small speaker as I took slow, deliberate steps toward Noah, my arm intertwined with Dad's. Marlene stood beside Noah with wet, shiny eyes and sniffled. I soaked in everything around me—the orange sun setting over the horizon, the sand between my toes, and the soft breeze blowing across my face.

When we reached Noah and Marlene, Dad lifted my veil and kissed my forehead. He shook Noah's hand and settled on my other side while Marlene reached down and turned off the music. We all shifted our attention to the officiant, a stocky, bald man dressed in all black.

"Good afternoon. We're gathered here today for the wedding of Noah Martin and Tracey Thompson. Noah and Tracey, as an expression of your total willingness to commit yourself to one another, please face each other and join hands."

Noah slipped his warm hands into mine and squeezed. With a gesture so simple, his love washed over me so completely that I couldn't help but feel like the luckiest girl alive.

The officiant continued. "Do you, Noah, take Tracey, to be your lawfully wedded wife, to have and to hold, in sickness and in health, to love, honor and respect, in good times and bad, for richer or poorer, keeping yourself solely unto her, for as long as you both shall live?"

"I do," he said.

"And, do you, Tracey, take Noah to be your lawfully wedded husband, to have and to hold, in sickness and in health, to love, honor and respect, in good times and bad, for richer or poorer, keeping yourself solely unto him, for as long as you both shall live?"

"I do." Wetness pooled behind my eyes at the same time that a smile tugged at my lips.

"Let us now have the rings brought forward."

I pivoted back toward the house. "Come here, Faith." Faith moved toward us, her head bowed and tail lowered. A little pillow was strapped to her collar, our rings tied securely to it. She sat in front of Marlene, just as we had practiced.

"Good dog," Marlene said as she unfastened the rings and handed mine to Noah.

"At this time, I invite Noah and Tracey to exchange the wedding vows they have chosen to write themselves."

Noah rested the silver band on the tip of my left ring finger. "Tracey, since the moment I laid eyes on you, even though we were only kids, I knew that I wanted you to be my wife. That feeling never wavered, and it only grows stronger with every single day. My heart will always be yours. Please take this ring as a sign of my commitment to love and honor you always. As this ring has no end, neither will my love for you."

The cool metal slid into place. I swallowed and tried not to get too emotional before it was my turn to speak. Marlene passed Noah's ring to me.

Preparing to recite the vows I had gone over so many times, I gazed up at Noah. It was hard to put into words how much I really loved him. I held the ring on the first knuckle of his finger. "Noah, even though we're still young, I'm absolutely sure that you and I are meant to be. I don't want to wait another minute to start our forever. Your love is my anchor, your trust gives me strength. With this ring, I pledge my life and my love to you. All that I am, I give to you."

I blinked away a tear as I pushed the ring down to its rightful place.

"By the power vested in me, by the state of New York, I now pronounce you husband and wife." The officiant's voice filled my ears, but I couldn't tear my gaze from the man I loved. "You may kiss the bride."

Dad and Marlene clapped.

Noah rested his hand on my cheek and leaned in. His soft lips brushed mine, lingering for a moment before he pulled away. "I love you," he whispered.

"I love you, too."

My husband. My heart filled with so much happiness I thought it might burst.

We walked back to our basement apartment hand in hand, Faith running ahead of us and through the doggie door, leaving Marlene and Dad standing with the officiant. Our honeymoon staycation had officially begun.

Day three of wedded bliss started much like the first two, with me and Noah wrapped in each other's arms. Untangling our limbs, I leaned over the edge of the bed to pick up Noah's shirt off the floor, slipping it over my head. He grabbed me around the waist and tugged me into him, my back pressed up against his solid chest. "Where are you going? Stay here with me." He peppered my neck with kisses.

"To get in the shower. We were planning to go out today, remember?"

"Do we have to?" He held me even closer. "I've got all I need right here." He nestled his head in the crook where my shoulder and neck met.

"I just want to join the land of the living long enough to get a good cup of coffee. We ran out yesterday morning."

He grumbled. "Fine, but only for a little while. I like being holed up in here with my wifey. I want you all to myself."

I turned my head and moved my lips over his. When I pulled myself out of his arms, he groaned in protest, and I couldn't help but giggle. "Don't worry. As long as you behave, I promise I'll make it up to you later."

One side of his mouth quirked up. "Well, then, what are we waiting for? Get showered and dressed woman."

We climbed into Old Blue, Noah's beat-up, old pickup truck. Even though the paint had faded over the years and rust dotted several spots on the bed, it didn't make Noah love it any less. He never talked about getting rid of the old vehicle, only about how he was going to make it better when he had the money.

"So, Mrs. Martin, where would you like to go first?"

Mrs. Martin. Warmth bloomed in my chest at the mention of my new title.

My stomach grumbled. "Want to get breakfast? We can grab bagels and coffee and then sit outside and enjoy the day." I peered out the windshield, noting the dark storm clouds hovering in the distance. "Or maybe just get breakfast and decide afterward. The weather looks iffy."

"Yeah. Is it supposed to storm? I haven't exactly been keeping up with the forecast. This new wife of mine keeps me too busy for that sort of thing." A wicked grin spread on his face and heat rose to my cheeks. I smacked him on the shoulder.

"Well, how would I know, being that I'm the one you're talking about?"

We settled at a small table at Murray's, a popular café in town and our favorite place to grab a quick bite. The news played on the television in the corner, where the meteorologist pointed to colored spots on the map. We couldn't hear what was being said, but we didn't need to. It grew more obvious by the second that it was going to rain buckets.

"So much for sitting outside today," I said.

"That's alright. I'm sure we'll find *something* to pass the time." Noah winked.

"Boy, this new husband of mine sure keeps me busy," I teased.

"Let's go." Noah laughed, crumpling up the stiff paper his bagel had been wrapped in, tilting his head toward the door. "I just thought of something we could do."

"Oh, did you?" I snorted. "Gosh, I wonder what that could be."

Giant drops splashed on Old Blue's windshield as we crossed town and headed back to the house. The wind picked up minutes later and heavy rain gushed from the sky, making it hard to see the road.

"Do you want to pull over?" I asked. "It probably won't keep up like this for long."

"I know these roads like the back of my hand. I don't think we need—"

"Watch out!" I shrieked. A small car crossed over the double yellow line and began to spin out of control, right toward us. Panic rose inside of me and another scream ripped from my throat. The car hurtled toward us as I sat helplessly in the passenger seat.

"Hold on!" Noah yelled. I grabbed on to the door handle just as he slammed on the brakes. Seconds before the other car would strike Old Blue, Noah cut the wheel hard to the right, as if he was timing it on purpose, trying his best to veer the truck out of the way.

The tires screeched before a loud crash boomed in my ears. I forced my eyes shut when the glass from the driver side window shattered and exploded through the interior, digging deep into my face and arms. The momentum of the other car threw my body sideways, lifting me out of the seat a few inches. I banged my head on something in the cab before the seatbelt locked and yanked me backward.

I didn't know how much time had passed when I finally opened my eyes. Sheets of water pounded on the windshield, which was broken but not busted through. Other than the rain, the cab of the truck was far too quiet. My heart started to pound. "Noah?"

My gaze drifted to the driver side. Slumped in an unnatural position, Noah's eyes were wide open, but they weren't fixed on anything. He wasn't moving, or talking. I covered my mouth with the back of my hand, trying to keep the sobs in, fear and disbelief consuming me at once.

"No," I cried out, freeing myself from the seat belt.

I wanted to unbuckle him, but I wasn't sure if that was a bad thing, knowing it sometimes could do more harm than good. I slid closer to him on the bench seat of the truck. My head pounded and my shoulder hung awkwardly from being out of joint. I didn't care though because Noah needed me.

I pressed my hand against his cheek, the coolness of his skin sending a chill up my own spine. Not a good sign. "Noah?"

No answer.

I placed my fingers on his neck to search for a pulse, but couldn't feel anything. I swallowed a strangled cry and moved closer despite my body's protests. Placing my ear to his chest, I prayed to hear the steady beating of his heart.

Still nothing.

This wasn't happening.

No.

My body shook as tears poured from my eyes. I glanced around the floor of the mangled truck for my phone but I couldn't see it. I was in bad shape and needed medical attention, but the will to help myself faded as the reality of what I had just lost sunk in. I curled up next to my reason for living, wishing I could have been taken with him.

When I walked into the viewing room at the funeral home, Noah lay before me in the black suit he wore to our wedding less than a week ago. The finality of his death kicked me in the chest again, the walls seeming to close in on me. I swallowed hard, kneeling in front of the casket, fighting to keep it together.

He looked so peaceful, like he could have been sleeping. Or, at least that would have been the case, had I not known that he never, ever slept on his back.

Too many thoughts swam through my head, too many regrets.

I'm so sorry, my love. This is all my fault.

Noah had wanted to stay in bed that morning. I was the one that had made him get up and I was the one that had made him leave with me, for a stupid cup of coffee, of all things. Why couldn't I have just been happy to be there with him? Had I not insisted, he would still be alive. The aching in my heart made it hard to breathe.

Marlene entered the viewing room, her eyes bloodshot. She tossed her purse on a chair and kneeled beside me, burying her face in her hands. Sobs racked her body almost instantly.

I rested my hand on her shoulder. "Marlene, I'm so sorry."

She had been through the tremendous loss of her parents before the wreck, when she was only eighteen, and she bore the brunt of the aftermath by raising her brother. Now that he was gone, she was the only one left. Worse yet, she and Noah had been as close as siblings could get.

The last thing I wanted was for her to feel like she was alone. Each time I tried to assure her that she wasn't, my words were either met with silence or hysterical, uncontrollable crying. Her pain tore me to pieces. The weight of her grief sat on my shoulders, because that, too, was my fault.

"Are you angry with me?" I asked, my voice sounding small in the large space. Maybe she blamed me for the accident as much as I did myself. If Noah and I had accepted her offer to send us on a trip for our honeymoon, we wouldn't have been home and the accident never would have happened. Rejecting her kindness and generosity had cost me Noah's life. Did she see it the same way?

The funeral director slipped into the room, closing the door behind him. "Ms. Martin, please let me know when you're ready to start receiving visitors. I don't want to rush you, but I thought you should know there's a line forming out the door. It's clear that Noah was adored by many."

Marlene wiped the tears from her face with the heels of her hands. She tried to catch her breath. "I just...need...a little more time... . alone...with my baby brother."

"Alright. There's no hurry. I'll come back in a few minutes." He left the room, closing the door behind him.

My eyes welled with tears. She had a right to have alone time with him. I could have kicked myself for not recognizing that need in the first place. "I'll leave you two for a little while."

Stupid and insensitive. Add that to my list of endearing qualities.

I stood and backed away, not waiting for an answer. Once I stepped out the rear exit of the room, I spotted the people waiting to pay their respects not too far off from me. The funeral director had not been exaggerating. The line went all the way down the hall and snaked around a corner, farther than I could see.

The mere idea of looking each of them in the eye, listening to their whispered words of condolence, seeing the pity on their faces—it was all too much. My knees buckled and my throat went dry. I braced myself against the wall.

I couldn't do it.

I inhaled deep, exhaling slowly, but it didn't help. Before anyone could notice my presence, I ducked into the coatroom. It was a safe place to stay hidden, considering it was the dead of summer. No one would have a jacket with them. I leaned against the wall in the darkness, wishing everyone would go away.

My phone buzzed, the caller ID popping up on the screen. *Dad.* I sighed. He was probably looking for me, and even though I didn't want him to worry, I couldn't bring myself to pick up the call. I waited for a minute until the message went to voice mail. When I hit play, Dad's broken, muffled cries hit me with so much force, even more weight pressed down on my shoulders and I sunk to the ground.

The whole situation seemed so unfair, not only for me, but for Marlene and Dad, too. We had already lost people close to us, people we loved beyond measure. Why did we have to lose another?

I didn't understand how I was supposed to go on. Life without Noah wasn't a life at all.

I slipped out of the coatroom and went left down the hallway, in the opposite direction of where everyone waited. When I reached the end, I pushed through an emergency exit, and kept on walking.

A glimpse of the sun peeked out on the horizon as the cool morning breeze pushed the curls away from my face. I zipped up my sweatshirt and pulled the hood over my head before sitting on the beach and burying my feet in the sand.

I settled in the exact spot where I promised Noah I would never stop loving him. It was the place where I felt closest to him, so I spent as much time as I could rooted to that specific patch of sand.

My heart hurt. I had lost track of how much time had passed since his death, and I didn't even care. Each useless day snowballed into the next, leaving me with nothing to do but miss him. Time didn't mean much to me anymore. As far as I was concerned, it was the only thing that stood between me and my love.

Faith emerged from the doggie door and trotted in my direction. She sat next to me, her gaze traveling over the water, her blue ball poking out from her mouth.

"Want me to throw your ball, girl?" I asked in a high pitched voice. "Give it here."

Faith grumbled before lying in the sand beside me. She dropped the ball and laid her head on top of it, soft whimpers escaping her throat. My chest tightened.

I stroked her soft, furry head. "I know, girl. Believe me, I know."

The sun rose higher in the sky, and clusters of people staked their claim on different areas in the sand, which was always my queue to leave.

As I re-entered the apartment from the beach with Faith on my heels, my phone vibrated on the kitchen counter, an unrecognizable number flashing up on the screen. I moved to answer it, but didn't make it in time. Unlocking the phone, I clicked on the voicemail message.

"Good morning, Tracey. This is Maria Jefferies calling from Synergy Inc. I apologize for the delay in following up with you. There have been some organizational changes since you came into the office, which has slowed down the recruiting process significantly. Both Brock and Peter thought that the interview went extremely well, but their budget has just been cut, so, unfortunately, we're unable to offer you a position at this time." Maria paused. "It seems like a case of poor timing. We're going to keep your resume on file and if an opportunity opens up that matches your qualifications, we'll reach out to you. Thanks for your interest."

Poor timing. That seemed to be the case for everything in my life.

Disappointment coursed through me, mingling with the bleak sadness that lingered always. I had been counting on that job. It was my ticket out of the basement apartment.

Every inch of space reminded me of the life I'd never have. Beyond that, I couldn't expect Marlene to keep a roof over my head, free of charge, indefinitely. My savings account was nothing to write home about, but it wasn't empty. Free loader didn't need to be added to my repertoire. I would start paying Marlene rent, and then when I landed a job, I'd be out of there.

I climbed the stairs and entered the kitchen. Marlene stood by the window over the sink, staring out at the ocean, a steaming cup of coffee in her hands. She glanced over her shoulder in my direction and then headed for the sliding glass door. "Faith, come!"

Faith galloped up the stairs from the basement apartment and nudged Marlene's leg. "Hey," Marlene said, surprise washing over her face. "Did you let yourself in through the doggie door again?"

Faith answered with a wag.

"Good girl," Marlene said, sliding the door shut.

"Marlene?" I took a seat at the kitchen table.

She pulled out the chair across from me and sat down, resting her large, red mug in front of her. Faith came up to Marlene, pressing the side of her body against the seat. "Such a poor lonely thing." She rubbed Faith behind the ears. "Yes, you are." Faith leaned into her hands with a satisfied grumble, one back leg thumping.

The fact that Marlene remained in the same room with me spelled progress. She had no interest in talking to me after everything had happened, and I couldn't blame her. Not when I blamed myself. But, her actions started to feel downright mean.

Didn't she understand that I was hurting, too? With Dad's constant traveling around the country for work, I, too, had no one. I would have thought we could have been there for each other.

"So." I cleared my throat. "I wanted to start paying you rent. It won't be much to start, but I feel the need to give you something."

She seemed to focus on the wall behind me, one eye squinting as if she was mulling over the offer. She shook her head and sighed.

Frustration gnawed at my insides. "What's with you? Are you ever going to talk to me?"

Marlene dropped her gaze to Faith, patting her on the head.

"You're not being fair. Do you know that?" I rested my hands on the table, balling them into fists. Enduring the silent treatment was no longer an option. If we had a problem, besides the obvious, it was coming out in the open. "Hey." I leaned over the table to grab her arm, knocking over her coffee by accident.

Both Marlene and Faith leapt out of the way. A look of confusion flashed over Marlene's face. She grabbed a wad of paper towels and started to sop up the mess. "Let's get this cleaned up."

"Sorry," I murmured, coming around the table to help.

Faith attempted to do her part also, licking up the other end of the puddle that Marlene hadn't gotten to yet.

"Stop that, you silly dog. " I shooed Faith away. She scurried out of the room and I turned the mug upright. "Marlene, hand me some of those paper towels, please. At least let me help you."

Marlene's eyes widened, her focus on the mug. "Faith? How did you—why'd you run?" Her gaze darted around the room. "What's wrong?"

"Nothing's wrong, but you know as well as I do that caffeine, and therefore coffee, is bad for dogs." I huffed.

She shook her head. "I must be going crazy." She continued wiping the floor, my words seeming to fall on deaf ears yet again.

"Can we please talk?" I asked.

Marlene tossed the mound of paper towels into the trash. "Faith, come." Faith came back into the kitchen, her head lowered. Marlene sat on the floor, and hugged Faith, drawing the big dog into her lap. She rested her head on Faith's. "You know what?" Her voice had dropped to a whisper. "Sometimes I wonder if they're still here. It's like I can feel them. When you run off like that, it makes me think you feel it too. Do you think they know how much I miss them?"

My mouth dropped open.

Them. Not him. But then that meant ...

No.

"Stop messing around, Marlene. Not only is that not funny, it's cruel." Marlene hugged Faith tighter, still not saying a word. I dropped in front of them, waving my arms around. "Talk to me, damn it."

Faith's head jerked up and she woofed, pushing Marlene to a more upright position. I reached out to touch Marlene and although she looked my way, she didn't say a word. I passed my hand an inch from her face, but she didn't even flinch, as if she couldn't even see me.

"Marlene!" I yelled so loud, I hurt my own ears. And still, it elicited no reaction whatsoever.

I gulped.

Not knowing what else to do, I ran down the stairs and paced the apartment, my heart pounding in my chest. Surely, this was some kind of horrible joke. Since Noah's death, my reclusiveness had been by choice. Hadn't it?

Memories flashed through my mind and the impossible reality slowly clicked into place.

First, the voicemails from Dad started to make sense. His heart wrenching messages filled with nothing but crying, and only one where he actually spoke.

I just wanted to hear your voice. I love you.

I hadn't tried to call him back because I couldn't be strong enough to listen to how much he missed Noah. But it wasn't Noah that he missed.

It was me.

And I hadn't thought of my friends all this time. I hadn't questioned why no one came around. I had assumed they all respected my wishes to be alone, that they had taken the hint when I never showed at Noah's wake or funeral. But now, it all made sense.

They never checked up on me, because they couldn't.

A strange comfort wrapped around me like a blanket, finally knowing that Marlene didn't hate me. I had been convinced that she did. Her behavior had been clawing away at my insides.

But, if I was truly dead, and Noah was too, where was he?

And more importantly, how would I find him?

The next morning brought fierce rain, reminding me all too well of the day of our accident. An image of Noah's lifeless eyes filled my mind, and I struggled to put the events of that day in order. The idea that I might never know and that I might be trapped in the solitude of this existence twisted my stomach in knots.

I stepped out into the deluge, not bothering to shield myself from the elements. By the time I reached my usual place, my hair plastered itself to the side of my face and my soaked clothes clung to my body. I dropped onto the wet sand and curled my arms around bent knees.

My sweet, loyal Faith popped out of the doggie door and sat next to me. She dropped her blue ball in front of her.

"You know I'm here, don't you, girl?" Her ears perked up and my heart squeezed tight. She was aware of my presence, but to what extent I didn't know. I wanted to find out. "Faith, speak."

She barked, swooshing her tail back and forth a few times.

"Now, give me your paw." I held out my hand.

When Faith's foot rested against my palm, grit from the beach combined with wet fur and grazed against my skin. Even though I couldn't understand what was happening, I took some solace in knowing I still had the unconditional love from my beloved pet. I wasn't completely alone. I released my hold and stroked her head. "You're such a good girl. I only wish you could help me. Do you know why I'm still here?"

Faith whined.

I breathed deep. "Yeah, neither do I."

Thunder rolled in the distance and lightning danced across the sky. The weather held no threat to me, but it wasn't safe for the dog to be outside. "Go inside, Faith." She didn't budge. I kissed her on her head. "Go," I commanded, my voice taking on a stern tone.

The dog whimpered, picked up her ball, and retreated toward the house. She hesitated at the halfway point, glancing back my way.

"Go. Now," I repeated, pointing at the house. She tucked her tail low, but she obeyed, disappearing through the doggie door. I pushed my hair away from my face and closed my eyes, lifting my head toward the sky. Lightning bolts struck over the water, thunder roaring even louder. "What do I do now?" I cried.

My eyes burned, and not before long, my tears mixed with the rain falling from the sky. I squinted, staring at the choppy waves sloshing against the shore.

"Where are you, Noah? I don't want to be here. Not without you."

A lightning bolt struck in front of me, a boom from the thunder ringing in my ears. Heat radiated off the sand, while a steady rumble vibrated on the ground. Holding up my forearms for cover, I tried to look ahead of me, only to be greeted with blinding flashes of light.

The noise subsided, and I let my arms fall away from my face. My jaw dropped. A bridge made of what seemed like smooth glass had formed where the water met the sand, arching upward into the sky. As I strained to see where the path led to, a figure emerged in the distance, running in my direction.

My heart hammered out of my chest as the person drew near. The familiarity of his gait, the broadness of his shoulders, the angles of his face—there was only one person it could have been.

Noah. My love.

Before I was aware of my own actions, my bare feet traveled over the wet sand and slapped against the smooth structure that led me back into Noah's strong arms.

The warmth of his embrace felt like home. It made me forget that we were standing in the middle of a raging storm, on a bridge suspended in midair. I grabbed his face with my hands and pulled him down to me, needing to feel his lips on mine. The contact made my insides tingle, happiness trickling back into my veins as I lost myself in the moment.

After a long while, Noah pulled away from our kiss, but he stayed close, brushing the line of my cheekbone with his thumb. His hazel eyes bore into me, charged with so much love, and so much life, that I filled with gratitude I never knew possible.

"I've missed you so much," Noah said, before pressing his lips to mine once more.

I threw my arms around his neck. "But all this time, where were you, while I was here?" I asked.

"Waiting for you."

"But I don't understand."

"I know." He nodded. "But you're getting close, and when you do, we'll get that forever we've always talked about." Hope shone in his eyes. "Let me help you."

I scrunched my eyebrows together. He took both of my hands and pressed them to his heart.

"Being with me right here, right now. How does this make you feel?"

I shook my head. "Like my world is as it should be. Whether I'm alive or not doesn't even matter. As long as I have you, the rest will fall into place. "

He pulled my hands upward and kissed one, then the other. "And when you were alone on the beach?"

My throat tightened. "Regret. Guilt. Hopelessness. Nothing good, in other words. Should I go on?"

Noah frowned. "You need to get to a place where you feel you can rest in peace. Let go of your regret. There's no need for it, no space for it where we're going. I never blamed you for what happened that day, Tracey. And neither did anyone else."

"But, I'm the reason why we left the apartment that morning."

"I don't recall you pointing a gun to my head and forcing me to go with you. Besides, I was the one who insisted we leave the café when we did. Do you remember what I was saying when we saw the car coming toward us?"

I shook my head.

"You had just finished suggesting we pull over until the rain let up. I was in the middle of saying we didn't need to. So, is it my fault then? Do you blame me?"

"What? Of course not." Some pressure lifted from my shoulders, but I couldn't let myself off that easy.

"What's going to happen to Marlene? We can't just leave her all by herself."

Noah's lips thinned. "Poor Sis. I don't want her to be alone, either. It breaks my heart to see her hurting."

I dropped my gaze, staring at the ocean that could be seen through the transparent floor.

Noah stuck two fingers under my chin and forced my eyes to meet his. "You know my sister is as tough as they come. She'll miss us, but she'll see us again. Her journey isn't over yet."

I nodded, hearing the truth in his words.

"This guilt, it's what's weighing you down and it's keeping us apart." He tucked a strand of hair behind my ear. "Forgive yourself." He took my face in his hands and kissed me one more time.

Confusion swirled within me. "That's really what's kept me here, all this time?"

Noah nodded.

My thoughts went back to when I regained consciousness after the car slammed into Noah's truck. I hadn't been able to piece the events together earlier, but if I wanted to resolve my feelings, I needed to understand how it all unfolded.

The memory gradually eased back into my mind. I had wrapped my good arm around Noah, tucking my head beneath his chin, wishing with desperation that I could have been taken with him. My head pounded, my shoulder throbbed. Each breath became harder to draw in, growing more and more shallow each time I tried to pull air into my lungs. Darkness crept in on the edges of my vision, and my consciousness faded. I invited the blackness, because the alternative was just as unbearable. The last words that had left my lips resonated in my mind.

If it weren't for me we would have lived happily ever after.

But I was wrong. We still had a shot at our fairy tale ending, and it wouldn't get away from me this time. The rain stopped falling and the sky brightened, as if the weather was trying to match my mood.

I stared up into Noah's eyes, a smile tugging at the corners of my mouth. "I think we need to renew our vows."

He raised an eyebrow, trying to keep a straight face. "But we just got married. What's your reasoning behind that?" he asked.

"They've expired."

He snorted. "Excuse me, Mrs. Martin? You're not getting out of being married to me that easily."

"The ones we said ended with committing to each other 'for as long as we both shall live.'"

A wide grin formed on his face, melting my heart.

"But we've proved our love is stronger than death. So, I'd like a do-over please. And next time, we can just say 'for eternity' instead, because I'm not losing you again. Not ever." I grabbed Noah's hand and tugged him toward the clouds. "Do they do wedding ceremonies in heaven?"

Noah broke my hold and draped his arm over my shoulder, leaning over to plant a kiss on top of my head. "Where we're going, anything is possible."

THE END

Turn the page for a sneak peak at the next story set in Mistport, NY. **Longing for Yesterday** is a sweet, contemporary romance novella which tells Marlene Martin's story. Happy Reading!

Bonus Material

Longing for Yesterday – Chapter 1

Marlene stood in her living room and glanced around, two baby carrots in her grasp. Her beloved golden retriever was nowhere to be seen. She never dressed for work so early, and her smart dog sensed something was up from the moment they went outside in the dark.

"Who wants a treat?" Faith's nails clicked on the hardwood floors, from the opposite end of the house. She appeared by Marlene's side, lifting her chin high enough to give the saddest eyes on the planet. Marlene rested a hand on her hip. "Come on. Don't look at me like that. I have your favorite this morning."

Marlene held out her palm. The dog's ears perked up and she rushed to the doggie bed to await her reward, tail wagging. Marlene crouched to set the carrots down and patted Faith on the head while she chomped away. "Don't worry, girl. Ellen is coming by in the afternoon to check on you. You'll be used to our new routine in no time." She straightened, grabbed her car keys, and headed out the door.

A new year, a new job. Life would be different, but this time, it would be a change Marlene sought out, and not one that came out of nowhere and crushed her.

But, before she took on a brave, new world, she needed a caffeine boost. She yawned as she pulled into Murray's, a popular coffee shop in town. Bells jingled and the glorious smell of fresh baked pastries filled her nose as she stepped through the entrance. Pine garland and red bows hung from the walls. The place bustled with activity. An employee took down a *Happy Holidays* banner in the far corner. Many of the tables were occupied. Some clicked away on laptops or read the paper, while others sat in small groups and talked.

A young woman stood at the counter, her dark hair tied back in a bun. She held a tray as she transferred croissants and muffins into the glass case beside her. "Good morning. How can I help you?"

"Hi. I'll have a large coffee, please. Cream, no sugar," Marlene said.

"Is there anything else I can get you?" The woman asked.

Everything. Marlene wanted to eat all of the things. It would be a dangerous, albeit delicious habit to fall into, though, eating pastries every morning on her way to work. She opted to stay strong, lamenting over a chocolate croissant on the inside. "No, thank you."

"Alright." The woman set down the tray and prepared the order. "That will be two dollars and twelve cents, please."

Marlene thanked her, paid for the coffee, and turned for the door. She paused to let another person inside, her mouth falling open as the man's midnight blue gaze locked on hers. She took a small step back. "Brady?"

Brady's brows knitted together as he pushed away dirty blond locks that nearly fell into his eyes. He sported a five-o'clock shadow that outlined his high cheekbones and the chiseled edge of his jaw. A black jacket stretched across his broad shoulders. Even through all the layers, Marlene could detect the outline of a lean, firm body.

Damn. Of course, he still looked good enough to lick. Marlene certainly didn't divorce him for being ugly.

"Marlene? You're out and about early," Brady said. Based on her old schedule, she'd still be roaming the house in her pajamas, which was no secret to her ex-husband. No harshness coated his tone, and no tension emanated in his stance, only what seemed to be a hint of surprise.

Marlene faked considerable interest in adjusting the plastic lid of her cup. Why did he have to be friendly, on the rare occasions they bumped into each other? If he acted like an ass, she'd be less likely to imagine throwing her arms around his neck and pulling him down for a kiss. Not that it mattered. He was never around when they were married, so no amount of lingering affection for him negated that fact.

"Yeah. Heading out to Warren. I'm starting work at a new company."

He tilted his head. "Really? That's over an hour away. I thought you loved your job."

Marlene shrugged one shoulder. "Time to move on."

Brady's face tightened. Marlene sensed the concern radiating off him, but she didn't need his pity or anyone else's.

"So, what brings you back to Mistport?" Deflection. Both an art form and a necessity for Marlene to operate in her small town. Two topics always came up, as if on repeat. Everyone either gave their condolences about her little brother Noah and his wife Tracy's tragic accident, or they told her what a shame it was that she and Brady couldn't work things out. While they may have had their hearts in the right place, Marlene hated rehashing the past with people who weren't even close to her.

He shoved his hands in his coat pockets. "I'm helping out Scott through his busy season." He flashed open one side of his jacket, revealing a blue shirt with a white emblem for his brother's oil delivery company, Nice Guy Oil.

Marlene noted his choice of words. Through busy season only—as in not here for good. Some things never changed.

"Trina is pregnant with triplets and on bed rest," he continued.

"Is she okay?" Marlene liked her ex-sister in law, but keeping in touch proved mega awkward. They had grown distant, but Marlene still wished the best for her.

"Yeah, she's nearing the end of her pregnancy and the doctor recommended she take it easy as a precaution."

"I'm glad it's not serious." She hesitated, not wanting to leave, but not understanding why either. "I've got to go, Brady. Take care."

His attention dropped to her lips, the way it used to right before he kissed her. Marlene's heart stuttered.

"You too." Brady held the door open for her. The woodsy scent of his cologne caught in her nose as she brushed past him. She ignored the tingling sensation from the faint contact. It wasn't like she got to enjoy his physical presence when they were together. She couldn't smell or touch a person who left her for three to twelve months at a time.

Yet another compelling reason to start over again.

Pick up a copy of *Longing for Yesterday* today!

About the Author

Melissa J. Crispin loves to mix things up by writing YA, Fantasy, and Romance. She spends her days in the corporate world, and pursues her passion for writing in the late nights and early mornings. When she's not working, she spends her time reading, listening to audiobooks, and binging TV shows that her two teenage kids say she's too old to watch.

Sign up for Melissa's newsletter to get updates on new releases.

Visit Melissa's website at www.melissajcrispin.com or connect with her online:

Facebook: facebook.com/melissajcrispinauthor

Instagram: @MelissaJCrispin

Twitter: @MelissaJCrispin

Also By Melissa J. Crispin

Collide (YA Fantasy)

The Crimson Curse (Sweet Fantasy Romance)

Longing for Yesterday (Sweet Contemporary Romance)